NBA

GAME DAY 2005

By John Hareas

SCHOLASTIC INC.

New York   Toronto   London   Auckland   Sydney
Mexico City   New Delhi   Hong Kong   Buenos Aires

PHOTO CREDITS

p. 3: (shoe photo) Jonathan Ferrey; p. 4-5: Jennifer Pottheiser;

p. 6 –7: Steve Babineau; p. 8: Bill Baptist; p. 9: Andrew D. Bernstein; p. 10: Randy Belice; p. 11: Scott Cunningham; p. 12: Bill Baptist; p. 13: Jesse D. Garrabrant; p. 14: Joe Murphy; p. 15: Andrew D. Bernstein; p. 16: Nathaniel S. Butler; p. 17: Al Bello; p. 18: Andy Hayt; p. 19: Jesse D. Garrabrant; p. 20: Bill Baptist; p. 21: Ron Hoskins; p. 22: Andrew D. Bernstein; p. 23: Rocky Widner; p. 24: D. Clarke Evans; p. 25: Noah Graham; p. 26: Garrett Ellwood, Allen Einstein (inset); p. 27: Brian Bahr; p. 28: Layne Murdoch; p. 29: Chris Covatta; p. 30: Andrew D. Bernstein; p. 31: Gary Dineen; p. 32: Jesse D. Garrabrant

ISBN 0-439-70399-9

Copyright © 2005 by NBA Properties, Inc.

All rights reserved. Published by Scholastic Inc.

SCHOLASTIC and associated logos are trademarks and/or registered trademarks of Scholastic Inc.

12 11 10 9 8 7 6 5 4 3 2   5 6 7 8/ 0

Printed in the U.S.A.   66

First printing, February 2005

Cover design by Louise Bova • Interior design by Rocco Melillo

NBA
GAME DAY 2005

The schedule is demanding. Eighty-two games over the course of six months. If a team is successful, the season will continue for another two months when an NBA champion is crowned. To deliver peak performance night in and night out, players need to stay healthy, practice (and practice and practice) while sticking to their routines. In *NBA Game Day*, go behind the scenes with some of the NBA's premier players as they prepare for an upcoming game. Grab breakfast with Shareef Abdur-Rahim as he catches up on the daily news in his hotel room. Hang out with Yao Ming as he works out with a medicine ball or be a spotter for Ben Wallace as he pumps iron only minutes before taking the court. You'll even walk along with LeBron James as he searches for his hotel room, which can be challenging with 41 regular-season games on the road! *NBA Game Day* provides fans with an all-access pass of what life is like for an NBA player in pursuit of the ultimate prize, the NBA championship. Enjoy the journey!

Fever Pitch

DEE-troit BAS-ket-balllll! Is there a louder arena in the NBA than The Palace of Auburn Hills in Michigan? Pistons fans don't think so. When the team's public address announcer—John Mason—whips the capacity crowd in a frenzy with the pregame introductions—

B-b-b-b-b-b-b-b-en
W-w-w-w-w-w-allace—

and flame shooters burst high above the baskets, it's also one of the most entertaining around.

Who Wants It?!

What time is it? Game Time! Opening tip—it is the moment of truth for every player who ever put on a basketball uniform. The countless hours of practice and preparation and endless drills all come down to this highly anticipated moment. Which players will step up? Who will hit the game-winning shot? Who will win? Who will lose? There is at least 48 minutes to find out.

Having a Ball

Is that the new official NBA basketball? No, it's actually a medicine ball that is bigger and heavier than a regular-sized basketball. Yao Ming uses this type of ball in building his stomach muscles during sit-up exercises.

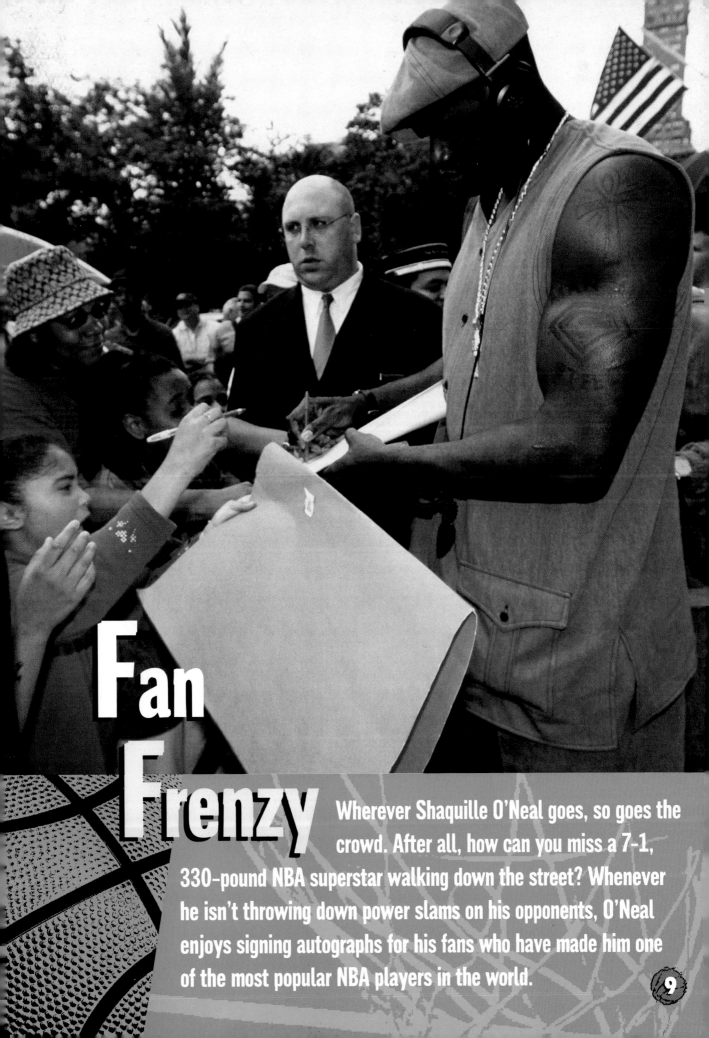

Fan Frenzy

Wherever Shaquille O'Neal goes, so goes the crowd. After all, how can you miss a 7-1, 330-pound NBA superstar walking down the street? Whenever he isn't throwing down power slams on his opponents, O'Neal enjoys signing autographs for his fans who have made him one of the most popular NBA players in the world.

Room 426 or 428?

Another day, another city: With 41 road games during a NBA season, which doesn't include the preseason or playoffs, it's easy to lose track of the day, time, even your hotel room number! LeBron James of the Cleveland Cavaliers didn't let the hectic traveling pace interfere with his on-court performance as he took home top rookie honors in his first season.

Energy Boost

When you're expected to run up and down the court for 40-plus minutes a night, getting a good start to your day is important. Shareef Abdur-Rahim relaxes in his hotel room with a bowl of oatmeal while catching up on the latest news.

Traveling Man

NBA teams often travel by bus to an opposing team's arena. The luxury carrier pulls up in the arena and allows players such as Jerry Stackhouse of the Dallas Mavericks close access to the locker room. The bus then waits until after the game to take the players back to the hotel or the airport for the next game.

Pumped Up

Part of Ben Wallace's pregame routine involves lifting weights in the locker room. The 6-9 power forward is one of the strongest players in the NBA and it's no secret as to why. His commitment to hard work has resulted in two back-to-back NBA Defensive Player of the Year Award and an NBA Championship. Not bad for someone who wasn't drafted by an NBA team.

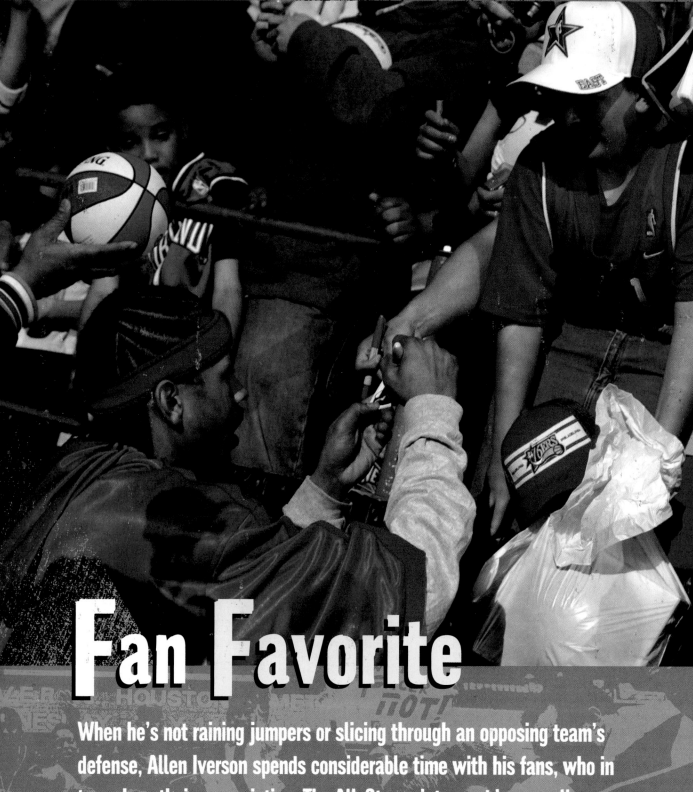

Fan Favorite

When he's not raining jumpers or slicing through an opposing team's defense, Allen Iverson spends considerable time with his fans, who in turn show their appreciation. The All-Star point guard is annually voted to the NBA All-Star Game and his jersey is among the league's best sellers.

Lets Go to the Tape

One of the more common pregame routines for many players is to have their ankles taped. Why? It helps reduce the chances of getting a sprained ankle. Tony Parker of the San Antonio Spurs always seeks treatment from the team trainer to ensure that he continues to blow by guards on the basketball court.

Next Question Please

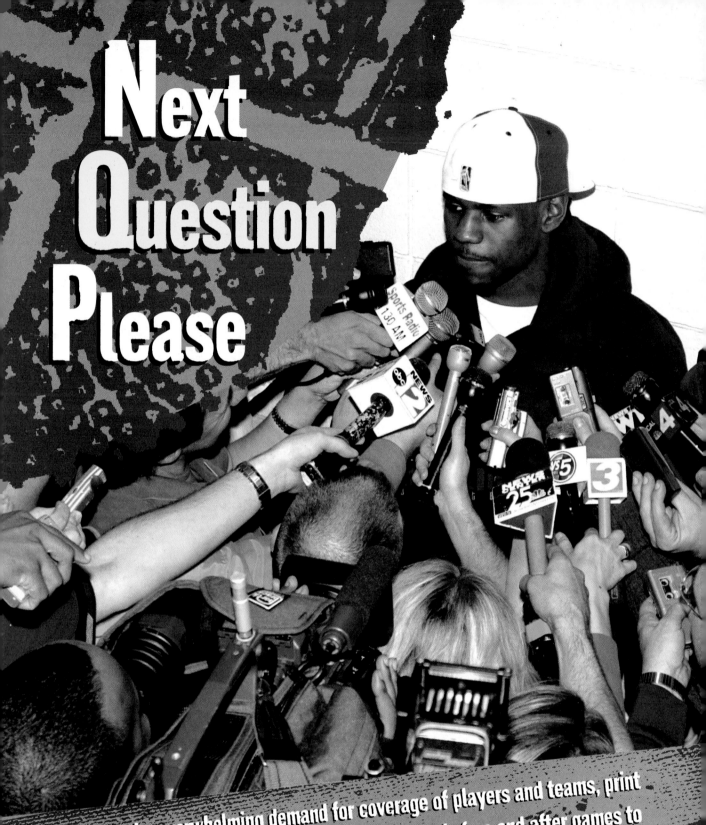

Due to the overwhelming demand for coverage of players and teams, print and broadcast journalists speak to NBA players before and after games to grab the latest news and updates. When a game is broadcast on national TV, players are also interviewed at halftime. LeBron James is not only popular with fans but, as you can see, he can certainly fill up a notebook.

Streeeeeeeetch

In order to assure peak performance, players must stretch before each and every game. Proper warm-up methods are crucial so players don't pull a muscle during a game. Players participate in a variety of drills and exercises before tipoff.

Game Face

Not only do players loosen up before each game (sometimes even with help from the team trainer), but they also prepare from a mental standpoint as Marko Jaric of the Los Angeles Clippers is doing here before a recent game.

Practice
Makes Perfect

Whether it is the 12th man off the bench or the team's No. 1 scoring option such as Allen Iverson of the Philadelphia 76ers, players take time to practice their outside shots before each game. It is this dedication that allows players like Iverson to help their teams to victory.

Bat Boy?

Wrong sport. Every NBA game is filled with nonstop action whether it's acrobatic dunks, spectacular shots and passes, and yes, sometimes even the element of the unknown. This ballboy tries to capture a bat that has somehow made its way into an NBA arena. No word if the bat paid for a ticket.

"Please Welcome, Your Indiana Pacers!"

The buzz in an NBA arena soon develops into a roar when the home team takes the floor for the first time. Electricity fills the air as all 12 members of the team begin their warm-ups in preparation of that day's game. As excited as the fans are, the players may be more so!

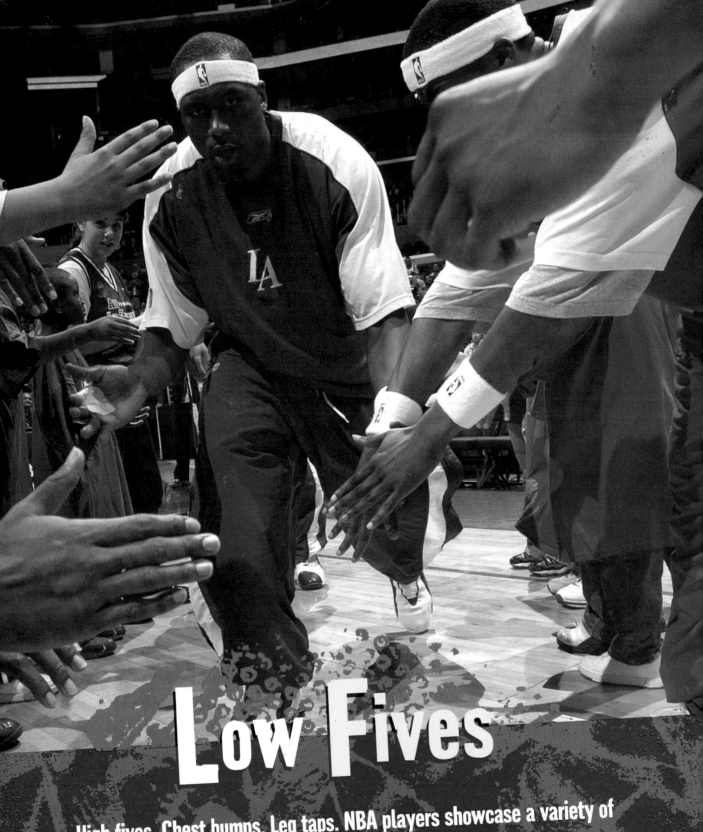

Low Fives

High fives. Chest bumps. Leg taps. NBA players showcase a variety of moves when their name is introduced in front of the hometown fans. The teams' public address announcer also takes the opportunity to shine with the unique pronunciation of some of the player's names.

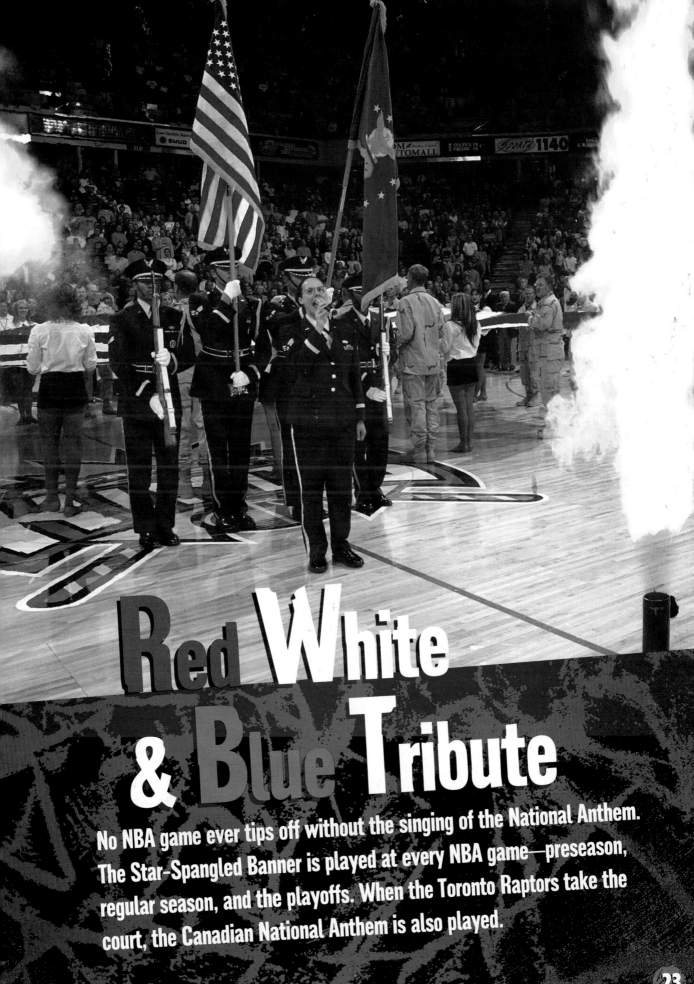

Red White & Blue Tribute

No NBA game ever tips off without the singing of the National Anthem. The Star-Spangled Banner is played at every NBA game—preseason, regular season, and the playoffs. When the Toronto Raptors take the court, the Canadian National Anthem is also played.

Focus

The calm before the basketball storm: Two-time NBA MVP and NBA champion Tim Duncan gathers his thoughts during the National Anthem before tipoff. Players have their own way of psyching themselves up before every game.

One, Two, Three...
Buzz

One way of showing team unity is by participating in the team huddle. Players gather to offer words of encouragement before tipoff. Some teams such as the New Orleans Hornets like to have fun by showcasing their moves before playing.

NOISE

Mascot Madness

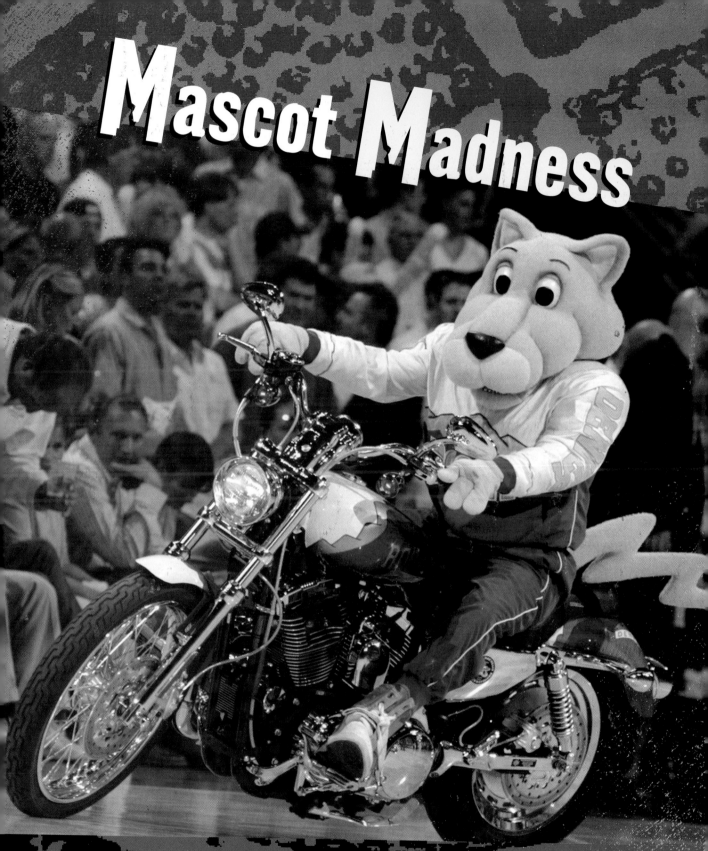

It's a bird . . . . It's a bear . . . It's a bull . . . It's a fox . . . It's—all of the above. NBA mascots come in a variety of shapes and sizes and entertain fans through-out the game. Dunking off a trampoline, riding a motorcycle, psyching out an opponent, you name it, the team mascot ensures fun for fans of all ages.

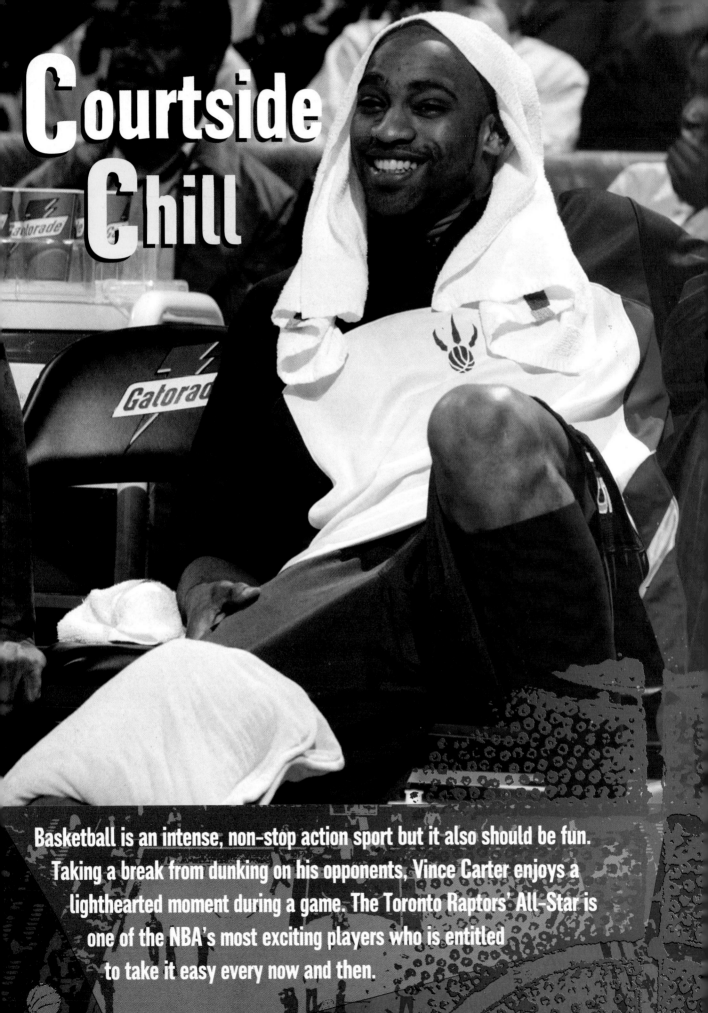

Courtside Chill

Basketball is an intense, non-stop action sport but it also should be fun. Taking a break from dunking on his opponents, Vince Carter enjoys a lighthearted moment during a game. The Toronto Raptors' All-Star is one of the NBA's most exciting players who is entitled to take it easy every now and then.

Fanatical
Devotion

Fans don't hold back when it comes to rooting for their favorite team. Some, such as this San Antonio Spurs' fan, want to show the world their deep devotion to their team. Painted faces, jerseys, and sometimes even wigs highlight the passion the fans display in cheering their team in person.

Full Moon

Not only are the Minnesota Timberwolves one of the NBA's premier teams, they also have some of the most loyal fans in all of sports. These fans showed their Timberwolves' pride at a recent game and help provide home-court advantage with their tremendous support. Ahoooooooooooo!

Team Unity

Teams such as the Milwaukee Bucks gather after games to regroup and talk about the big victory. Unfortunately, teams can't win every game but regardless of the win-loss record, it's extremely important to stay united as a team.

31

Championship
Celebration

Richard Hamilton waves to fans after the Detroit Pistons win the
2004 NBA Finals against the Los Angles Lakers on June 15, 2004.